Dear Reader,

This book was made completely by me, Jake Cake. I did all the words and all the pictures and it took me ages. It's about all the strange things that get me into trouble. Strange things that are SO STRANGE no one EVER believes me.

When I try telling grown-ups what REALLY happened they shake their heads and say: 'DON'T MAKE UP STORIES OR YOUR NOSE WILL GROW LONG!' But I'm not making up stories. Every thing I'm about to tell you is true. It all REALLY HAPPENED!

Signed Jake Cake

Michael Broad spent much of his childhood gazing out of the window imagining he was somewhere more interesting.

Now he's a grown-up Michael still spends a lot of time gazing out of the window imagining he's somewhere more interesting – but now he writes and illustrates books as well.

Some of them are picture books, like *Broken Bird* and *The Little Star Who Wished*.

Books by Michael Broad

JAKE CAKE: THE ROBOT DINNER LADY
JAKE CAKE: THE SCHOOL DRAGON
JAKE CAKE: THE VISITING VAMPIRE
JAKE CAKE: THE WEREWOLF TEACHER

JAKE CAKE

THE VISITING VAMPIRE

MICHAEL BROAD

PUFFIN

*This book is dedicated
to my friend Ness*

PUFFIN BOOKS

Published by the Penguin Group
Penguin Books Ltd, 80 Strand, London WC2R 0RL, England
Penguin Group (USA) Inc., 375 Hudson Street, New York, New York 10014, USA
Penguin Group (Canada), 90 Eglinton Avenue East, Suite 700, Toronto, Ontario, Canada M4P 2Y3
(a division of Pearson Penguin Canada Inc.)
Penguin Ireland, 25 St Stephen's Green, Dublin 2, Ireland (a division of Penguin Books Ltd)
Penguin Group (Australia), 250 Camberwell Road, Camberwell, Victoria 3124, Australia
(a division of Pearson Australia Group Pty Ltd)
Penguin Books India Pvt Ltd, 11 Community Centre, Panchsheel Park, New Delhi – 110 017, India
Penguin Group (NZ), 67 Apollo Drive, Rosedale North Shore 0632, New Zealand
(a division of Pearson New Zealand Ltd)
Penguin Books (South Africa) (Pty) Ltd, 24 Sturdee Avenue, Rosebank, Johannesburg 2196, South Africa

Penguin Books Ltd, Registered Offices: 80 Strand, London WC2R 0RL, England

puffinbooks.com

First published 2007
1

Copyright © Michael Broad, 2007
All rights reserved

The moral right of the author has been asserted

Set in Perpetua
Made and printed in England by Clays Ltd, St Ives plc

Except in the United States of America, this book is sold subject to the condition that it shall not, by
way of trade or otherwise, be lent, re-sold, hired out, or otherwise circulated without the publisher's
prior consent in any form of binding or cover other than that in which it is published and without a
similar condition including this condition being imposed on the subsequent purchaser

British Library Cataloguing in Publication Data
A CIP catalogue record for this book is available from the British Library

ISBN: 978–0–141–32090–8

Here are three UNBELIEVABLE stories about the times I met:

A Vampire...........page 1

Two Demons..........page 47

And a Knight........page 93

JAKE CAKE

AND THE

Visiting Vampire

Sometimes we have visitors at our school who spend the morning with the class to tell us about something interesting, or at least it's supposed to be interesting. One time we had a farmer who spent the whole morning going on about potatoes – which was really boring.

You might think
it would at
least be good
to get away
from teachers
for a bit, but
the teachers stay in the classroom
the whole time. They sit in the
corner, keeping an eye on
everyone to make sure
we don't give the visitor
a hard time.

When the farmer
visited I fell asleep in
class and started snoring
like one of his pigs. Mrs
Grump obviously hadn't

forgotten this because after introducing Mr Graves she took a seat beside the whiteboard and spent most of her time watching *me*.

Mr Graves stood at the front of the class. He was very pale and wore a long black cape and a black top hat. Mrs Grump introduced him as a magician – which probably meant he did card tricks and pulled rabbits out of hats at little kids' parties.

oops!

YAWN!

Mr Graves took off his top hat and started rummaging around inside it.

I was expecting him to pull out a rabbit, or a string of coloured handkerchiefs. So I was as surprised as the rest of the class when he stopped rummaging, whacked the bottom of the hat and out flew a huge cloud of bats!

A couple of girls screamed, Mrs Grump's mouth fell open and everyone else gasped in amazement as the bats began circling the room, flapping and screeching loudly.

This was *definitely* better than potatoes!

Mr Graves clapped his
hands together twice and the bats
gathered over his head in a big black
flapping cloud. Then, with a click of his
fingers, they all disappeared in a great
puff of purple smoke!

The whole class started
clapping and cheering; even Mrs
Grump was clapping. She didn't
cheer, but she did seem to be smiling
which is not like Mrs Grump at all and
looked very odd!

'Vunderful!' said Mr Graves, with a

funny accent. 'I have your attention!'

Mrs Grump continued to clap after everyone else had stopped, until the magician frowned at her and she quickly put her hands back in her lap. I've never seen my form teacher get so excited before, which probably should have tipped me off that something was wrong.

'For my next feat
of magic I vill
need a volunteer,'
said Mr Graves.

Everyone immediately
put their hands up, even Mrs
Grump. I was the only one
who didn't because I was
troubled by what I saw
in the reflection of the
window.

Actually, I was more
troubled by what I
couldn't see.

It was grey and cloudy outside so the whole bright classroom was lit up in the reflection of the glass. I saw Mrs Grump, I saw Mrs Grump's desk and the whiteboard, I saw all the other kids with their hands in the air (including me *without* my hand in the air), but I couldn't see Mr Graves at all!

The magician had no reflection!

When I turned
back Mr Graves was
looming over me,
which gave me
a massive fright.
I'd been so busy
looking at the
class through
the window I
hadn't seen him creep up
to my desk.

'YOU!' said the
magician, pointing a pale
bony finger at me. 'You vill
assist me vith my next
amazing illusion!'

GULP!

Under the watchful glare of Mrs
Grump I reluctantly made my way to
the front of the class with Mr Graves.
I glanced in the window one more time
to make sure I hadn't imagined the
magician's missing reflection. No, there
I was, walking alone
with a very worried
look on my face.

I quickly made a
list in my head:
Pale skin.
A hat full of bats.
A black cape.
A dodgy accent.
No reflection!
A VAMPIRE!

me making a list
in my head

Everything definitely pointed to a
vampire, but they can't come out during
the day or else they turn to dust (even if
it is dull and cloudy). So Mr Graves had
to be something else.

The magician stood at the front of
the class and handed me a long silver
chain with an old-fashioned watch on
the end.

'Hold this up and sving it from side to side!' he demanded.

'Sving it?' I said, not knowing what he meant.

'Yes, sving, sving!' he snapped, waving his hand backwards and forwards.

'Oh, you mean *swing*?' I said.

'Yes, sving!' he growled. 'That's exactly vhat I said!'

SVING!
SVING!
with a
funny
accent

I held the
chain up and
let the watch
swing from
side to side, because I couldn't see what
harm it could do. And while Mr Graves
told everyone to gaze at the *vatch* and
surrender their *vill* (I think he meant
watch and *will*), I looked around, trying
to find clues to discover who or what
he was.

There was a black rucksack under
the desk. So while Mr Graves was busy

Mr Graves Rucksack

BOOT!

telling the
rest of the
class to concentrate on
the watch, I inched my way forward and
booted it.

The rucksack fell over and a plastic
bottle rolled out and landed at my feet.
As I read the label my eyes
widened.

It was a bottle of
suntan lotion.

Factor 60!

Complete sun block!

FACTOR
60
COMPLETE
SUN
BLOCK

I dropped the chain, took a deep
breath and yelled at the top of my voice:
 'THE MAGICIAN ISN'T REALLY
A MAGICIAN, HE'S A VAMPIRE
AND HE HASN'T TURNED TO
DUST BECAUSE HE'S WEARING
LOADS OF SUNTAN LOTION!'

Now, usually when I shout out something like that (which happens quite a lot), the other kids start screaming, or they laugh because they think it's funny, or I get told off for making up stories. Sometimes the other kids scream *and* laugh, *and* I get told off all at the same time.

But this time nothing happened!

I looked around and saw my classmates staring at me with wide vacant eyes. Then I turned to Mrs

19

Grump, who I was sure would have
something to say about my outburst, but
she was staring at me with
wide vacant eyes too.

I waved at Mrs
Grump to get her
attention but she
didn't even blink!

'MWAH HA
HA!' boomed the
vampire, throwing

his arms up and flapping his cape dramatically (vampires are well known for flapping their capes around dramatically. I think they think it's scary, but it just looks silly).

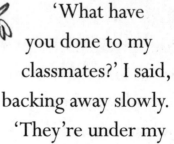

'What have you done to my classmates?' I said, backing away slowly. 'They're under my spell,' hissed the vampire.

'What do you want with them?'
I asked, trying to buy some time so I
could work out how to get away.

'I vill make them my slaves, of
course!' said Mr Graves. 'My castle in
Transylvania is very large and doesn't
look after itself, you know!'

'So you *are* a vampire!' I said,
because vampires usually live in
Transylvania.

Mr Graves nodded.

'But what about Mrs Grump?' I said.
'She's too old to be a slave.'

'Hmmm,' said the vampire, eyeing
Mrs Grump up and down with a frown.
'I think your teacher will be my new
manservant,' he said. 'My last one had
an unfortunate accident and I've been

looking for a
replacement.'

'But she's
not even a man,'
I said, not really
knowing what a manservant was but
guessing they'd probably have to be a
man to get the job.

The vampire considered this,
took a marker pen from the desk and
wandered over to Mrs Grump. He
leaned down and drew a big black curly
moustache on my teacher's top lip.

'There, that's better,' he said,
stepping back to admire his handiwork.

Mrs Grump looked really funny with a curly black moustache drawn on her face, but I didn't have time to enjoy it because something else was worrying me.

Mrs Grump was going to be a manservant with a marker-pen moustache.

The other kids in my class were going to be slaves.

Which left only one person.

'What about me?' I said, edging back until I bumped into Mrs Grump's desk.

The vampire scratched his chin thoughtfully and then smiled, baring his big ugly fangs for the first time.

'I vill drink your BLOOD!' he boomed. 'MWAH HA HA HA!'

The vampire's red eyes suddenly widened and so did his mouth. Then he flicked his cape up in the air and swooped down on me like a big black eagle swooping on a rabbit!

I couldn't get away because he was too quick and I was trapped against the desk, so I reached around and grabbed the first thing I could lay my hands on.

Mrs Grump's register!

I shut my eyes tight and swung the book as hard as I could!

WHACK!
I'd definitely
hit something
because when I
peered out through
one eye I saw two things at once. The
first was the vampire with
his mouth open, looking
very surprised and very
gummy. The second
was a pair of fangy false
teeth flying through
the air like a missile,
and landing on the

floor with a clatter.

The vampire was stunned
for a moment so I dropped
the book, ducked past him and, because
a vampire without fangs can't bite you,
I quickly grabbed the teeth before he
could shove them back in again.

Then I scarpered out of the
classroom as fast as my legs would
carry me.

As I bolted down
the corridor I heard
running footsteps
and a cape
flapping behind
me. I glanced
back just in

time to see the vampire leap into the air! Suddenly there was a loud bang and a cloud of purple smoke, and out from the smoke flew a very large angry bat.

'ARRRRRGGGGH!' I screamed, but then came up with an idea.

I skidded to a halt at the end of the corridor and held my breath as the bat flapped and screeched towards me.

But just as it swooped down, I shot into the boys' toilets and slammed the door shut behind me.

THUD!

The thud was immediately

followed by the squeaking sound of a bat sliding down the other side of the door.

I ran to the nearest cubicle, threw the teeth down the toilet bowl and flushed the chain. As the teeth gurgled away I looked at my hand and noticed the slimy vampire drool dangling from my fingers.

YUCK!

After washing my hands I opened the door slowly and looked down.

VAMPIRE DROOL

DAZED BAT!

There was a dazed gummy bat gazing up at me from the floor, and because a dazed gummy bat isn't very scary, I picked it up by one of its wings and dragged it back to the classroom.

Mrs Grump was still sitting in the corner of the room wearing a

DRAG

marker-pen
moustache and
gazing into space
(which was a bit
of an improvement
because she
wasn't moaning
or glaring at me).
The other kids
in the class were

all still gazing silently at the whiteboard
(which would have pleased Mrs Grump
if she hadn't been sitting in the corner
of the room wearing a marker-pen
moustache and gazing into space).

Everyone was obviously still under

the vampire's spell, and because the
vampire bat was still under the spell of
the toilet door, I heaved him on to the
desk, took a seat and waited.

Eventually
there was a half-
hearted bang

and a thin cloud of purple smoke, and as
the smoke drifted away Mr Graves the
vampire was sitting on the desk looking
like he'd been dragged through a hedge
backwards.

'MWAH HA HA HA!' I said,

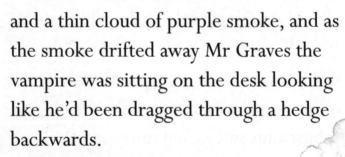

because I couldn't help myself.

The vampire looked very angry.
He jumped off the desk and stood over
me, flapping his cape dramatically. But
without his teeth he didn't
look scary any more; in
fact, he looked a bit silly.

'Vhere are my . . .'
he demanded, but I
interrupted him.

'I flushed them down the toilet,'
I said.

The vampire gave a defeated sigh,
and then looked around the
CLICK!   room.

'Vell, I still have your class
and your teacher!' he laughed,
picking up his rucksack and
putting the top hat back on his
head. 'I vill have them carve me
a bigger, sharper set of teeth and then I
vill come back for *you*!'

The vampire raised
his hand and clicked his
fingers together.

Suddenly the whole
classroom stood up at
the same time, including

Mrs Grump, and stared at Mr
Graves expectantly, waiting for
his instructions.

The vampire sneered at me
(which isn't easy to do without
teeth), turned towards the door and
clicked his fingers again. Mrs Grump
and the whole class followed him,
staggering from behind their desks like
zombies.

GULP!

I'm always in trouble at
school for losing homework
or library books, so I knew I'd
be in DEEP trouble if I lost my
whole class *and* my teacher. Even
I wouldn't believe that a vampire had
taken them to his castle in Transylvania,
so I had to stop them myself.

I had an idea.

As the whole class was about to
leave the classroom I raised my
hand and clicked my fingers
together.

CLICK!

Suddenly all the
zombies stopped and
turned to face me,

which was a bit creepy,
so I quickly clicked
my fingers again and
everyone went back to
their seats!

The vampire spun
around angrily and snapped his fingers.

Everyone immediately stood up
again.

I snapped my fingers and everyone
immediately sat down again.

The vampire snapped his fingers and
everyone stood up again.

I snapped my . . .

Well, you get the idea. This actually
went on for quite a while and all

the time Mr
Graves was
getting angrier
and angrier.
Eventually he
lurched towards me, and
although he still didn't have any teeth
the vampire suddenly looked very scary
again!

I jumped out of my seat to get away
and trod on something small
and hard that immediately
smashed under my
feet. The vampire
froze and looked a

SMASH!

bit worried, and when I
looked around I could
see why.

The whole
class, including
Mrs Grump, had
woken from the
spell.

Glancing down I saw the silver
watch I'd dropped earlier. Breaking it
had obviously broken the spell because
everyone, including my teacher, was
looking very confused.

'What on earth is going on here?'
yelled Mrs Grump.

'THE MAGICIAN ISN'T REALLY A MAGICIAN, HE'S A VAMPIRE AND HE TURNED EVERYONE INTO ZOMBIES AND I FLUSHED HIS TEETH DOWN THE TOILET!'

At least this outburst got a reaction, but not the one I'd hoped for.

Mrs Grump looked angrier than I'd ever seen her before

ARRRGGHH!

(even angrier than the
time an ogre ate her desk
– but I'll tell you about that another
time).

She was about to tell me off when I
suddenly realized I had proof!

'He hasn't got a reflection!' I said,
before Mrs Grump could speak. 'Look
in the window!'

Mrs Grump narrowed her eyes and
turned towards the window.

'ARRRRRGGGGGGHHH!' she
screamed, and turned back to face me
with a look of horror on her face.

'You see,' I said. 'I told you. Mr
Graves is a vam–' I glanced around and
noticed that Mr Graves had gone!

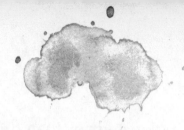

He must have legged it while everyone was watching Mrs Grump.

So why had Mrs Grump screamed if the vampire had already scarpered?

Had my teacher seen something else in the glass, something much worse than a vampire, some hideous monster that the vampire visitor had conjured up before fleeing the scene?

As Mrs Grump glared at me I realized the answer was written on her face.

My teacher had seen her marker-pen moustache!

GULP!

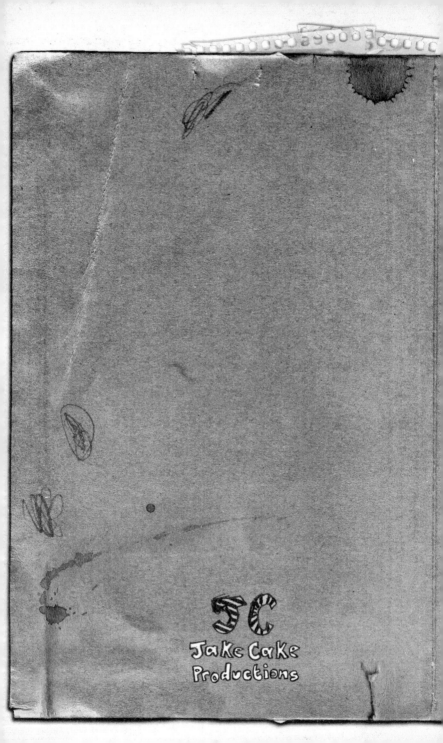

JC
Jake Cake
Productions

JAKE CAKE
AND THE
DEMON HAIRDRESSERS

If you don't hurry up we'll be late for your appointment!' Mum snapped, grabbing my arm and pulling me along beside her.

She'd rumbled my plan.

I thought if I shuffled slowly enough
we'd be late for the hairdresser's and
have to make a new appointment. *Then*
I'd have time to come up with a proper
scheme to get out of it, like I usually do.

Mum had been sneaky this time. I
didn't know about the haircut until she
pounced on me at the school gates,
and by then it was too late. I'd walked
straight into a haircut-trap and there

was no time to leg it or come up with a decent escape plan.

Mum *always* gets my hair cut the way she likes it, neat and nerdy with a side parting, and it takes ages to get it looking scruffy again. I'd managed to dodge the last three appointments, but now my luck had finally run out and I was doomed to be the least cool kid in school.

My appointment was at the Saloon
Salon, a Wild West-themed hairdresser's
that Mum thought would be fun. And
it would have been fun too, if I hadn't
been there to get a nerdy haircut.

Mum watched me carefully as we sat
in the reception.

SCRATCH
SCRATCH

I scratched my scruffy head and
thought hard.

I decided the last chance I had to
escape the scissors was to pretend
to head for the chair when my name
was called, and then quickly change
direction and scarper out the door.

'Jake Cake?' said the hairdresser,
stepping through swinging saloon doors.

I was about
to put my last-
minute escape
plan into action
when Mum
leapt from her
chair like a
jack-in-the-box,
blocked the
door and folded
her arms defiantly.

'He's here,' she said with a wry smile.
'And he would like nice and neat with
an adorable side parting.'

As the hairdresser led me away Mum
gave a triumphant sigh.

She must have been
planning this for weeks!

The hairdresser was very tall and
thin, with a long nose and very bushy
eyebrows. Her assistant was short
and round, with a pointy nose and no
eyebrows at all. They were both wearing
scissor-holsters and Stetsons.

I sat in the chair and watched through the mirror as the hairdresser and her assistant peered at my hair.

'Hmmm,' they said together, moving in for a closer look.

Glancing up, all I could see were two sets of hairy nostrils twitching as the pair exchanged frantic glances,

TWITCHING
HAIRY
NOSTRILS

whispers and angry grunts over my head. And from where I sat it sounded like they were arguing about who would cut my hair.

'Mine!' snapped the hairdresser.

'Mine!' snapped the assistant.

'This one is MINE!' the hairdresser growled. 'You can have the next one!'

The assistant fell silent and stuck out her bottom lip.

'I don't mind who does it, so long as it's not neat and nerdy,' I said hopefully.

The hairdresser and her assistant frowned at each other as though they'd completely forgotten there was a person sitting beneath the messy mop of hair. They turned their heads slowly and peered at me through the mirror.

'We're not deciding who gets to *cut* it!' hissed the hairdresser.

'We're deciding who gets to *keep* it afterwards!' hissed the assistant.

'Oh,' I said, shrinking back down in the chair.

My eyes darted between the hairdresser and her assistant as they continued their argument. Something *very* strange was going on right above my head, but I couldn't work out what

SHRINKING
BACK DOWN
↓

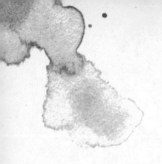

it was. Who were
these hat-wearing
hairdressers and
why were they
arguing over who got
to keep my scruffy old
hair clippings?

'Mine!' snapped the hairdresser,
poking the assistant in the chest.

'Mine!' snapped the assistant,
twanging the hairdresser's long nose.

'Mine!' snapped the hairdresser,
prodding the assistant's pointy nose.

FLICK!

Suddenly
the assistant
reached up
and flicked off
the hairdresser's
hat, revealing a shiny
bald head with *two small
horns sticking* out of it! The hairdresser
gasped and retaliated, flicking off the
assistant's hat and revealing another
shiny bald head with *one stumpy horn* in
the middle (like a baby rhinoceros)!

I immediately knew what I was
dealing with.

DEMONS!

Demons are *everywhere* if you know what to look for. I once found one living in our chimney! I chased it out with a poker and got into loads of trouble for getting soot everywhere (but I'll tell you about that another time).

One thing you need to know about demons is that aside from being really, really ugly, they're also really, really stupid.

These two were so stupid they hadn't realized I'd seen their horns and they didn't even notice when I slipped out of the chair and legged it. And I would

have escaped too, if Mum hadn't been patrolling the exit.

'But they're DEMONS!' I pleaded, as Mum continued to block the door.

'So, it's *demons* now, is it!' she sighed, rolling her eyes. 'Honestly, Jake! All this fuss over one little haircut!'

I was about to carry on pleading when I heard frantic footsteps approaching and the demons appeared with their hats crammed on at awkward angles. They glared at me with mean demon eyes and

then quickly became flustered when
they saw Mum.

'Oh, I'm terribly sorry, Mrs Cake,'
said the hairdresser.

'The little rascal just wriggled away!'
added the assistant.

'Don't worry, I was expecting an escape attempt,' Mum said, nudging me back towards the demons. 'Perhaps I should come in and keep an eye on him while you cut his hair?'

'NOOOOO!' boomed the hairdresser angrily.

Mum looked startled and the demons exchanged worried glances.

'NOOOOO charge!' added the assistant hastily.

'Excuse me?' said Mum.

'NOOOOO charge for haircuts today,' said the assistant, who was now looking up at Mum's hair with wide greedy eyes. 'It's a special promotion we're having for ladies with pretty hair!'

'Pretty hair?' Mum smiled, glancing in a nearby mirror and fiddling with her fringe. 'You think I have pretty hair?'

'*Very* pretty hair,' said the assistant, and drooled.

'Well, maybe I could use a *little* trim.' Mum chuckled, obviously flattered by the compliment. 'If it's not too much trouble?'

'No trouble at all,' grinned the assistant.

'But they're DEMONS!' I sighed.

'Now that's quite enough of that,' Mum said, leading me back into the salon. She plonked me down in the chair and eyed me through the mirror. 'And I'll be watching you the whole time, so behave yourself,' she warned.

GULP!

While the demon
assistant combed
and snipped Mum's
hair at the other
end of the salon,
the demon
hairdresser
scratched her chin
with one hand and prodded my messy
mop with the other.

'What do you want with the hair
anyway?' I said, because I was curious.

'I'm going to chop it all off and glue
it on to my head!' said the hairdresser,
as if it was the most normal thing in the
world.

'Er, why?' I asked with a frown.

'Because my hat keeps falling off,' said the demon matter-of-factly.

'Oh,' I said. She was much too fierce to argue with.

I should have worked it out earlier. Demons are well known for dressing up as humans. They steal clothes from washing lines and usually wear 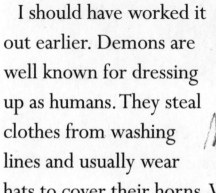 hats to cover their horns. Wigs make them itch, which is always a dead giveaway, so I guessed real hair was the next best thing.

The hairdresser was still scratching her chin when the assistant came over to us.

Through the mirror I saw Mum still

sitting at the other side of the salon. She was now under a big hairdryer, reading a magazine.

I hadn't seen exactly what the assistant had done to Mum's hair, but she seemed happy enough.

Mum saw me looking and waved – it was a slow I'm-still-watching-you wave.

GULP!

'My new hair is going to look *very* pretty when it's set!' said the assistant, jumping up and down excitedly. 'And

when I've chopped it all off and glued
it to my head, I will look *much* prettier
than you!' she added, sneering at the
hairdresser.

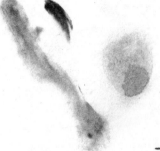

The demon
hairdresser glared at
the assistant.

'Wanna bet?' she
snapped.

As the assistant
skipped away to a room
at the back of the shop, the hairdresser
began working frantically on my messy
mop with her long bony fingers. With
grim determination she scooped and
groped and twirled handfuls of hair,
sculpting and shaping it like a big crazy
bird's nest.

Mum occasionally peered over her magazine at me, but she was obviously just making sure I hadn't scarpered. She paid no attention to the terrible things that were happening on top of my head!

The demon curled some of my hair into ringlets and braided other bits into plaits. There were a couple of bunches on top of my head and other bits just sticking up all over the place.

Finally, when every hair had been dealt
with, the demon hairdresser grabbed a
massive tin of hairspray and squirted a
big stinky cloud of it all over my head.

She stepped back to admire
her handiwork.

I scowled in the
mirror at the
horrible hairy
sculpture on
my head.

But, looking on the bright side,
I decided there was nothing worse she
could do because there was no more
hair left to do it with.

'Hmmm,' said the demon, looking
around the salon.

Suddenly the hairdresser smiled
as she spied a large display of
hair decorations – bows and
ribbons and plastic flowers.

GULP!

Wheeling the whole display case over
to my chair the demon began sticking
the bows and ribbons and plastic flowers
on to my hideous hairdo. She crammed
on as many as possible, grinning like
a mad thing as my head grew heavier
and heavier.

Eventually she stepped back again to survey her creation.

'Perfect!' she hissed.

I looked in the mirror at Mum, hoping she'd notice the massive girly mess on my head and demand to know what was going on, but she'd fallen asleep under the warmth of the dryer.

So much for keeping an eye on me!

With Mum fast asleep I suppose I could have legged it, but that would have meant running down the high street with THAT on my head, which wasn't really much of an option. In fact my hair was so scary I would have happily shaved it all off just to get rid of it – but I didn't much like the idea of a demon running around with my hair glued to her head!

There had to be another way.

The demon approached the chair again, smiled an evil smile and drew a set of buzzing hair clippers from her holster!

BZZZZ!!

'Time to harvest my pretty new hair!' she squealed excitedly.

As the demon hairdresser leaned in to shear off my hair, I looked around frantically.

Then I peered into the sink in front of me and suddenly had

an idea. Quick as a flash I grabbed the shower head, held it up to my head and curled my finger around the trigger . . .

WOOOOOSSSHHHHHH!

The ringlets and plaits were blasted out of my hair by the huge jet of water, quickly followed by the bows and ribbons and plastic flowers. They shot off my head one by one and splattered the startled demon.

'ARRRRRGGGGHHH!' she screamed.

Although I think she was mostly screaming at the state of my hair.

The scream caused the assistant to come running from the back of the shop. She was holding a gooey paintbrush and had already covered half of her horny head with glue!

When she saw the soggy hairdresser and my soaking mop, the demon assistant began screaming too, although *she* was screaming with laughter.

GLUE↓

The demon hairdresser turned around slowly and flared her hairy nostrils.

'ARRRRRGGGGHHH!' she screamed again, but this time with anger.

Suddenly the hairdresser leapt into the air and landed on the assistant's back! To hold on she clasped her hands around the gluey horn on the sticky head and immediately stuck fast.

In the Stetson the
demon hairdresser
looked like a
cowboy riding a
baby rhinoceros.
The pair crashed
around the
Saloon Salon
stuck firmly
together, wailing and growling wildly.

Which I have to admit was very funny
to watch.

Then I realized I wasn't the only one
watching.

Mum was gawping at the demons
with her mouth hanging open. She
immediately turned to me and
narrowed her eyes — and I'd seen that

look before. It was the look that meant I was about to get blamed for everything!

Mum stepped out of the hairdryer and stormed over to me.

'What on earth have you been up to?' she demanded.

I was about to blurt out something about demons gluing hair on their heads, but then I stared up at Mum with a very worried look on my face.

'Er, Mum . . .' I said.

'What?' she snapped, annoyed that I was changing the subject.

'Have you looked in the mirror?' I said.

'Have I looked in the mirror?' She frowned. 'Well, no, but . . .'

Mum's eyes caught her reflection and her jaw immediately dropped.

'ARRRRRGGGGHHHH!' she screamed.

Now demons *are* pretty scary — but they're nowhere near as scary as Mum when she's angry. And when Mum looked up and saw her large,  frizzy, frazzled hair in the mirror she became madder than I've *ever* seen her before (meaning she was REALLY mad)! While Mum was busy swinging her handbag

mum Swinging her handbag.

at the heap of wrestling demons, I quickly combed my wet hair to make it look neat and nerdy with a side parting, and tucked all the scruffy bits away behind my ears.

It looked very uncool.

I turned back just in time to see the two terrified demons running out of the door as fast as the assistant's short legs would carry them.

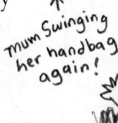

↑
mum Swinging her handbag again!

It seemed no amount of hair was worth getting a battering from Mum and they continued to leg it all the way along the high street (which must have startled a few shoppers!).

Mum took a deep breath, pulled on her coat and shouldered her handbag.

'We're leaving!' she said calmly.

Crossing the Saloon Salon I looked down and saw a Stetson; it had dropped from the demon rhino-rider as she ducked through the doorway.

I picked it up and offered it to Mum.

'You could put this on for now?' I
said, frowning at Mum's scary hair.

Mum looked at the hat, glanced at
her hair once again in the mirror and
quickly crammed it on her head.

'Well, at least you look tidy, pardner,'
she sighed, patting my damp head.

If Mum realized I'd dodged the nerdy haircut, she didn't say anything or make another appointment for me, not for a while anyway. She was far too busy making appointments to sort out her own demon hairdo!

PHEW!

Of course Mum didn't know she'd done battle with two demons – she thought she'd done battle with two very bad hairdressers. But either way Mum had rounded up the demons, and run them out of town.

And I wasn't the least cool kid in school.

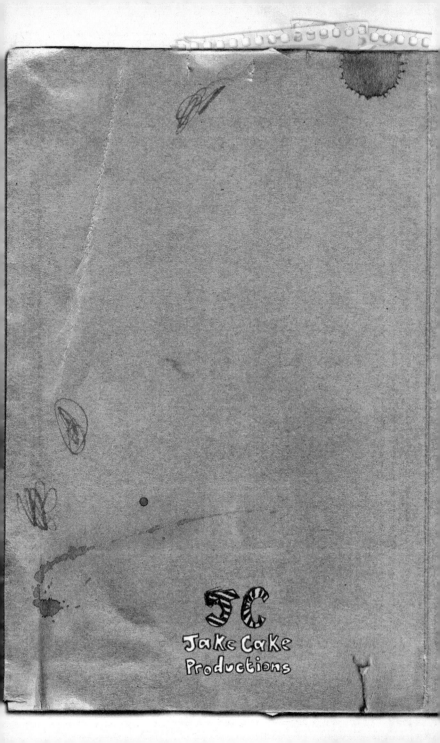

JC

Jake Cake
Productions

JAKE CAKE

AND THE

HAUNTED CASTLE

Mum and Dad usually take me to the beach during the summer holidays. *This* year Mum refused to go because she said it held too many painful memories, and she still didn't feel comfortable showing her face there.

'And you can take that look off your face right now, young man,' she snapped, eyeing me through the car's rear-view mirror. 'You have no one to blame but yourself!'

The truth is that last year I got into loads of trouble with a sand monster and it all ended with me, Mum and Dad being escorted from the beach by the police because

they said I was terrorizing the other holidaymakers (it wasn't me, it was the sand monster, but I'll tell you about that another time).

This year we were going to stay in a castle for the weekend, which did sound fun – but not as much fun as snorkelling in the sea. So I made a point of sulking in the back of the car for the two whole hours it took to drive there.

When we arrived I continued to sulk
because the castle turned out to be no
fun at all! No dungeons, no suits of
armour and nothing at all for kids to
do. It was like a big castle-shaped hotel
with no TV. And because it was in the

middle of nowhere, I couldn't even nag
Mum and Dad to take me into town to a
cinema or an arcade.

So I was stuck for the whole weekend
with nothing to do.

On the first day nothing much
happened.

Mum wandered around the castle
grounds and got really excited about the
rose bushes. Dad followed Mum with
a guidebook, pointing out statues and
other things that
were supposed
to be interesting.
While I trailed
along behind both
of them yawning as
loud as I could.

By the end
of the day Mum
said she'd had just
about enough of
my sulking. She
said if I wasn't
interested in all
the wonderful
historic things
in the castle then I might as well go to
bed – and sent me to my room.

And *that's* when things *finally* got
interesting.

I was sitting on my bed reading by
torchlight (because I wasn't tired and
there was nothing else to do) when
I heard a strange noise coming from
under the bed.

I closed my book and listened carefully until I heard it again.

Clang, Clang, Clang!

Because it wasn't a *growling* sound or a *screaming* sound (which would have been really scary – especially in a creepy old castle), I leaned over the bed and shone

my torch underneath to find out what it was. But there was nothing there

except a few balls of fluff on the dusty
stone floor, and balls of fluff don't make
clanging sounds (in fact I don't think
balls of fluff make any sounds at all).

I shrugged and was about to leave
it when I heard the noise again, but
this time the fluff balls moved with
a draught and I could see something
sticking out of the floor.

Climbing down I reached under the
bed, swept the dust away and found
a small piece of
rope attached
to an old
trapdoor!

I'd like to say
I took a moment
to think
about it and
considered *not*
investigating
the noise, so
I could stay
out of trouble
(especially after what happened
on the last holiday). But I was SO bored
I didn't see that I had much of a choice.

I pulled on the rope and the door
creaked open.

Propping the trapdoor
open with my book, I slid
under the bed on my belly. Shining
the torch down the dark hole in the

floor I saw narrow stone steps leading to a passageway that ran directly under my room.

CLANG, CLANG, CLANG!

The sound made me jump; it was much louder with the door open and it seemed to echo through the passage. I was tempted to shut the trapdoor and forget all about it. It was very dark and *anything* could be lurking down there.

CLANG! CLANG! CLANG!

But then I remembered how bored
I'd been all day and decided a bit of
exploring was just what I needed.

It was probably just some rusty old
pipes clanging anyway.

As I reached the bottom step I stopped
and pointed the beam of light down the
passageway (just to make sure nothing
was lurking). It seemed to go on forever
and my torch wasn't bright enough to

see what was
up ahead, but
I was already
down there and
decided to go a
little further just
to see where it
went.

It felt like I'd been
walking for ages
when the narrow
passage took a sharp
bend to the left, and
turning the corner
I discovered a large
wooden door ahead
of me.

CLANG, CLANG, CLANG!

I jumped back with fright and dropped my torch, and as it hit the stone floor I heard the bulb crack and the light immediately went out!

GULP!

Looking around I was surprised to find the tunnel wasn't pitch black as it should have been. There was light coming from the other side of the door, flickering through the keyhole and between the gaps in the wood.

GULP!

I guessed I'd probably found a
tunnel that led to the castle kitchen
or something boring like that, and the
noise was probably just the clanging of
saucepans. So I stepped up to the door
and peered through the
keyhole.

Well, it definitely
wasn't the kitchen!

I hadn't actually
seen the castle's
kitchen, although
I was pretty sure it
would have electric
light bulbs like the
rest of the castle, and this room was lit
with two flaming torches in iron holders
on the wall!

I couldn't see much else through the keyhole and still had no idea what was making the clanging sound, but I also didn't want to go back the way I'd come without my torch.

I took a deep breath, lifted the latch and pushed the door open.

Suddenly a tall metal figure lurched across the room in my direction swinging a giant axe!

'ARRRRRGGGGGGHHH!' I
screamed as the axe thunked into the
wood above my head.

I gazed up at
the knight in
shining armour
(although the
armour wasn't
very shiny
– it was dull
and dusty and
looked rusted
around the
joints). But the
knight didn't
look down. In fact
I think he *couldn't* look down because
the neck of the armour was so rusted.

Which meant he probably hadn't even seen me.

As I suspected the knight just pulled the axe from the door and lurched off in the opposite direction,

crashing into furniture along the way. He didn't seem able to bend his knees either, so he looked like a great metal zombie.

The room
appeared to be a
dining hall. It had
a long wooden table
with metal plates and cups
on it, but there was no food on
them and everything was covered in
dust and thick stringy cobwebs. There
were shields and tapestries on the walls
and racks of spears and swords at
one end.

'Hello?' I yelled, as the
knight crashed into the wall
with a great big CLANG!

The knight was about to lurch in another direction when he stopped suddenly and shuffled around to face me (which took him quite a while).

'Are you an actor?' I said, because Dad had mentioned that sometimes actors came to the castle, dressed up in old-fashioned clothes and put on medieval shows for the guests (Mum said she'd like to be a damsel in distress, whatever that is).

'Mmmf mmm mtttthhhh!' the knight said, although I couldn't understand what he was saying because everything was muffled inside his helmet.

'Eh?' I said, moving closer. 'I can't hear you.'

'Mmmf mmm mtttthhhh!' the knight mumbled again impatiently. This time he was trying to point to his helmet and the effort nearly made him topple over.

With a closer look I could see all

RUST

MORE RUST

the hinges on the helmet had rusted
shut and the grille across the front was
blocked up with dust and cobwebs. He
obviously couldn't see *anything* which
explained why he was lurching around
and bumping into things.

I suddenly realized an armed knight
who couldn't see what he was doing
wasn't a good idea, so I yanked the
axe out of his hand and put it down on
the table (it was really
heavy and landed with
a thud).

GREASE →

OLD RAG ↓

A grumbling sound came from inside the helmet – but I ignored it. I told the knight to stay where he was and went over to the rack of spears and swords to find something to prise the helmet open. Instead I found a tin of grease and an old rag, which was even better.

Pulling a stool over to the knight I stepped up and started rubbing away the rust with a big dollop of grease. It took a while but eventually I managed to free the grille part of the helmet and flipped it up.

'ARRRRRGGGGGGHHH!'
I screamed, and fell backwards off the
stool.

I had no idea who or what I would find
inside the helmet – but I'd definitely
expected to find *something*! Instead what
I found was nothing but a few stringy
cobwebs.

The knight didn't have a head!

Thinking about it, the
CLANG, CLANG,
CLANGING sound
had been pretty
hollow – which
meant he probably
didn't have a
body either!

So I did what any sensible person would do – I legged it in the direction of the tunnel, not caring any more how dark it was!

Suddenly the knight spoke in a strange tinny voice that seemed to vibrate and echo around his armour.

'I do beg your pardon,' he said. 'It was not my intention to give you a fright.'

I stopped before reaching the door and glanced back.

The knight was

waving at me; at least his helmet was
pointing in my direction and his metal
glove was creaking from
side to side, which
seemed
friendly
enough. And
he wasn't
holding an axe
any more so
there wasn't any
real reason to be
scared.

'CREAK CREAK'

'Are you a ghost?' I said,
because when you're not sure
it's always best to ask.

'Um, yes,' said the ghost.
'I suppose I am.'

'Then why can't I see you?' I said. Because I've seen ghosts before and this was the first ghost I'd seen that I couldn't actually see!

The suit of armour shrugged as best he could, which didn't look much like a shrug and was very noisy as metal rubbed against metal.

I was now more curious than scared of the ghost I couldn't see, so I went back over to get a closer look. Standing back up on the stool I held the sides of the metal helmet and peered inside.

'Hellooooooo?' I called into the empty armour, and my voice echoed through his belly and limbs.

'Please don't do that,' said the knight, and his voice was so close to my head it made me jump.

'Sorry,' I said, realizing that shouting into his armour was probably quite a rude thing to do.

'Do you think you could rub some of that grease on my

joints?' said the knight. 'I seem to have rusted up since they stopped cleaning me and it has restricted my movements somewhat.'

'Can't you just step out of the armour?' I said, because ghosts can usually walk through walls and stuff, so I couldn't see the armour being much of a problem.

'Unfortunately, no,' said the ghost, pulling the face grille back into place with a clang. 'I'm somehow attached to it. Some ghosts have a whole castle to haunt, while *I* appear to be stuck with this wretched suit of armour.'

'Can't you haunt the castle *in* the armour?' I said, dolloping grease on the metal knees and elbows and working it in with the rag to free them up. 'That would be cool! Especially if you carried the axe with you!'

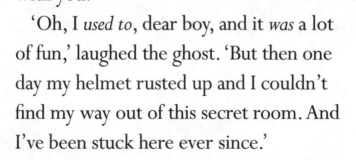

'Oh, I *used to*, dear boy, and it *was* a lot of fun,' laughed the ghost. 'But then one day my helmet rusted up and I couldn't find my way out of this secret room. And I've been stuck here ever since.'

'People must have heard you trying to get out,' I said. 'I heard you.'

The suit of armour shrugged again, but this time it looked like a proper shrug because his elbows and shoulder joints were moving freely.

The ghost gave an excited gasp.

'I can move!' he said, reaching his

oops!

arms high in the air and swinging them around (which reminded me of when Mum does her aerobic exercises). 'Thank you so very much. Is there anything I can do to return the favour?'

'Well . . .' I said, scratching my head and pretending to think about it, although I immediately knew what I wanted. 'There is *one* thing you could do, if you don't mind.'

'I am your humble servant,' said the knight, bowing freely.

'We have to get you out of here

SCRATCH SCRATCH

SCRATCH
SCRATCH

first, though,' I said.
The suit of armour
looked around at
the walls, scratched
the top of his helmet
with his metal-
fingered glove and then
led me over to the wall. He counted the
stones while nodding his head from side
to side and then stepped forward.

'I can't walk through walls!'
I gasped.

'Neither can I,' said the knight. He
reached forward and pushed one of
the stones, which slid into the wall.
Suddenly a whole section of wall
creaked open like a giant stone door.

'I've been trying to find that brick

for years!'
sighed the
knight.
'But with
my grille
clogged up,
I couldn't
see a thing.'

Which
definitely
explained all
the CLANG, CLANG, CLANGING!

Suddenly I remembered
something and quickly
ran back to the table.

'You'll be needing
this!' I said, grabbing
the axe.

The secret door led into the main hallway of the castle and luckily there was no one around to see us. They would definitely have got a fright if they'd seen a knight with an axe stepping through the wall.

I led the knight carefully up the stairs and along the corridor until we reached the door of my parents' room.

'If you could just burst through the door and wave your axe around in the air, that would be great,' I whispered.

'No chopping?' asked the knight.

'NO!' I gasped. 'No chopping *at all*!'

The knight nodded.

'OK, I have to go to my room and pack my bags now,' I said, patting the knight on the shoulder. 'It was very nice meeting you.'

'You're leaving the castle?' the knight said, and sounded disappointed.

I glanced at the door to Mum and Dad's room.

'I think I will be very soon,' I smiled, and then legged it down the corridor.

From my room I
first heard the screams,
followed by the yells,
followed by running
footsteps and the sound of Mum
and Dad hammering on my door.

I grabbed my rucksack and stepped
out into the corridor.

'WE'RE LEAVING!' gasped
Mum and Dad together.

'Oh, I was just
beginning to enjoy
myself!' I said.
'Castles are *full*
of cool stuff!'

'Well, you'll
just have to
make do with

the beach instead!' Mum
snapped, grabbing my arm
and dragging me down the
corridor. 'And I don't want to
hear another word about it!'

'OK,' I said, smiling to myself.

Mum and Dad hurried me down the
stairs and out through the entrance
hall, where I saw the
knight standing against
the wall. The
castle staff were
all gathered
around
him and the
manager was
rubbing his
chin.

'Where on earth did he come from?' he said to the cleaner.

'I have no idea,' said the cleaner, flicking over the knight's armour with a feather duster. 'But first thing tomorrow morning I'm going to give him a really good polish!'

Dad shielded Mum's eyes as they passed the knight, and as I tagged along behind I saw him give a tiny wave with his metal gauntlet.

Tiny Wave

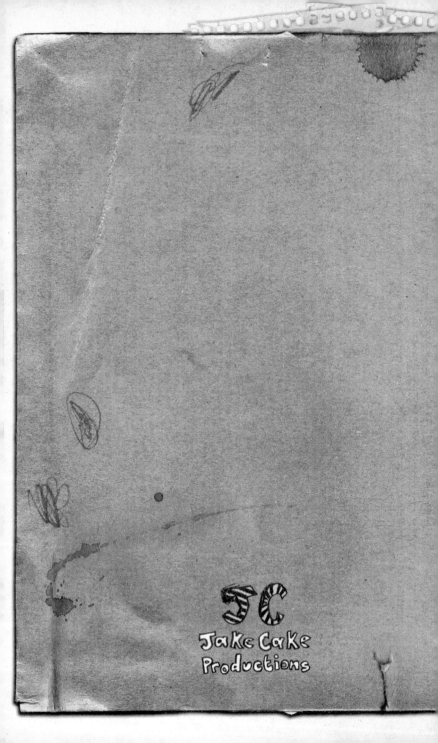

JC
Jake Cake
Productions

UNBELIEVABLE ADVENTURE REPORT

NAME: Mr. Graves. (vampire)............

AGE: ..very old. (the un-dead usually are)...

WEIGHT: ..not very heavy when they're bats-
I know because I had to drag Mr Graves
along the corridor-phew!

How To Spot One. pointy teeth and a dodgy cape
(and look out for sun block in the
daytime!)

Comments: Vampires are not very nice-and
they have a thing about turning
people into zombie slaves, so I
think vampires are probably very
lazy.

IF they swing an
old-fashioned watch
at you...
DON'T LOOK AT IT!

JC
Jake Cake
Productions

UNBELIEVABLE ADVENTURE REPORT

NAME: DEMONS!!! (didn't catch their names).

AGE: doesn't matter how old they are - demons of all ages are very

WEIGHT: I think the mean! short round one weighed more than the tall thin one!

How To Spot One. HORNS!!!

Comments: Demons are ~~very~~ horrible and they are always trying to look like humans. Keep an eye on your washing line because one day a demon will show up and try to steal your clothes! Also-

Jake Cake
Productions

Demons are VERY STUPID! he he!

UNBELIEVABLE ADVENTURE REPORT

OFFICIAL JC DOCUMENT

NAME: Knight (I forgot to ask his name)...

AGE: Hundreds of years old! ..... Sorry.

WEIGHT: The ghost probably weighed nothing - but the suit of armour weighed a TON!

How To Spot One: Go to a castle and listen for a CLANG! CLANG! CLANG!

Comments: The Knight was very nice and friendly - I was actually sad to leave the castle because we could have had a lot of fun. But SNORKELLING was BRILLIANT so I don't regret giving mum and Dad a

JC
Jake Cake Productions

KNIGHT FRIGHT!
he he!

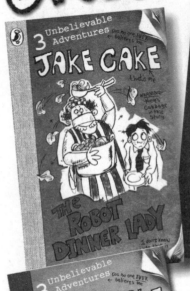